# The Year of the Ranch

By Alice McLerran
Illustrated by Kimberly Bulcken Root

VIKING

The illustrations were done in pencil and watercolor.

VIKING Published by the Penguin Group
Penguin Books USA Inc., 375 Hudson Street, New York, New York 10014, U.S.A.
Penguin Books Ltd, 27 Wrights Lane, London W8 5TZ, England
Penguin Books Australia Ltd, Ringwood, Victoria, Australia
Penguin Books Canada Ltd, 10 Alcorn Avenue, Toronto, Ontario, Canada M4V 3B2
Penguin Books (N.Z.) Ltd, 182–190 Wairau Road, Auckland 10, New Zealand

Penguin Books Ltd, Registered Offices: Harmondsworth, Middlesex, England

First published in 1996 by Viking, a division of Penguin Books USA Inc.

1  3  5  7  9  10  8  6  4  2

Text copyright © Alice McLerran, 1996
Illustrations copyright © Kimberly Bulcken Root, 1996

LIBRARY OF CONGRESS CATALOGING-IN-PUBLICATION DATA
McLerran, Alice.    The year of the ranch / Alice McLerran; illustrated by Kimberly Bulcken Root.    p.    cm.
Summary: In 1919 Papa, Mama, and their four daughters homestead a tract of land near Yuma, Arizona,
and try to turn a desert mesa into farmland and a shack into a home.
ISBN 0-670-85131-0
[1. Frontier and pioneer life—Arizona—Fiction. 2. Arizona—History—Fiction.]
I. Root, Kimberly Bulcken, ill. II. Title. PZ7.M47872Ye 1996 [ E]—dc20 95-46308 CIP AC

Printed in Singapore    Set in Stempel Schneidler

To Pete
and to the memory of César
—A. M.


To Ernest and Marian Linker
with love
—K. B. R.

"The desert shall rejoice, and blossom as the rose!" Papa's voice rang above the rattling of the car.

Emily watched Mama. Mama was sitting very straight, not taking her eyes from the ruts that showed where the road was. "John," she said, "for five years now we've had a house with a flush toilet."

Her voice sounded odd and tight. Almost as if she were going to cry, thought Emily.

"My father tried farming out on the mesa," Papa persisted, "and until the flood of 1891 he did fine. Our land is higher."

Mama lifted her chin a little but didn't say anything more. Finally the car turned off the road and labored up a sandy slope. "Here we are," said Papa. He went around to let Mama out, and the four girls climbed out of the back. Papa stood with his arm around Mama as she looked at the place he had built. Everyone was quiet.

"Are we going to have to live out here?" asked Jane finally.

Mama turned. "Papa and I will need to be here—sleep here—for three years," she said carefully. "That's part of what we have to do if we want the homestead office to give us the land, free. And Papa has to put in a well, and plant crops. Those are the rules for a homestead. But Papa will still keep his job at the office. The rest of us could stay in town at Auntie Irene's during the day, at least for now. You girls could sleep there while Papa and I sleep here." She paused. "Or we could all try living here right away. That's what Papa and I have to decide."

Emily was staring at the shack. It was just a patchwork of old lumber. It didn't look big enough for six people.

Maybe Papa read her thoughts. "I could add a sleeping porch along the front," he said. "We'd wake up to that view of the mountains."

"There's no bathroom?" said Jane.

Mama took a deep breath, and pulled Jane close. "When I was a girl we lived for a time on a ranch," she said, "and we had a tennis court. John, do you suppose we could lay out a court here for the girls?" So Emily knew it was decided.

While Papa and Uncle Alf built the sleeping porch, Mama helped the girls scrape the stones from their tennis court. Papa put up a net, and bought a wheeled machine to mark out the lines with white lime. By the time the family was ready to move in, Jane and Carol were learning to hit the ball back and forth. Emily and little Helen raced after the balls the older girls missed.

On moving day a lot of furniture had to be left behind in the house, but Papa and Uncle Alf managed to fit the piano onto the truck, for Mama. Mama wrapped the silver tea service from Grandma Van Kleeck in a quilt, and carried it on her lap in the car.

Supper the first night was late; Mama had a hard time getting the kerosene stove to work. She kept humming all the time she was cooking, so Emily knew she'd better behave. Humming didn't mean Mama was happy. When she was happy she sang.

After supper, while Mama washed the dishes in water carried from town, Papa took the girls for a walk to the top of the mesa. Emily held his hand as they stood in a row, looking down across the bare slopes of their own land and into the valley beyond. Off in the distance, a line of mesquite and cottonwood trees marked where the Gila River flowed west to join the Colorado. In the last rays of sunlight, the mountains were blue and purple and magenta.

"The desert shall blossom as the rose," repeated Papa. "Someday we'll be able to lead the waters of those rivers in through the dry land, and this whole valley will be a garden." As he spoke, the shadows in the valley seemed tinged with green. Emily was proud to be there with Papa, seeing it all with him.

One thing kept bothering her, though. She couldn't help asking about it when Mama was tucking her into bed. She whispered, so as not to worry the others. "Papa hasn't ever been a farmer. Can he really get things to grow here? There isn't even any water."

"Of course he can," Mama whispered back. "Your father is a very capable man." She kissed Emily. "Anyway, the Prests have the land right next to ours. Mr. Prest will help. Everything's going to be all right."

Before breakfast that next morning Mr. Prest had come over and was putting in the pump for the well. As soon as Papa had finished his coffee he led everyone out to see how Mr. Prest was doing. "Ho, everyone that thirsteth, come ye to the waters!" proclaimed Papa. "Ted, need a hand?"

Mr. Prest wiped his forehead and looked up. Papa was dressed for the office in his three-piece suit. "Thank you kindly, John, but I think it's about done."

Little by little, they learned the tricks of living there. Scorpions liked to come up on the screen windows in the evening, and so did tarantulas and vinegarroons. Emily invented a system. She and Mama would get two flatirons. Emily would wait indoors next to the screen while Mama, humming bravely, tiptoed outside. On signal, they clapped their irons together and flattened the invader. Everybody cheered but Mama.

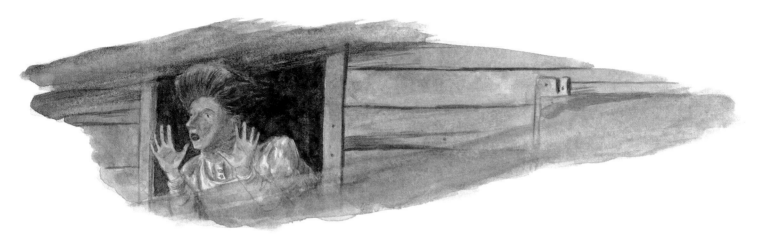

Like sailors at sea, they had to keep an eye on the weather. When a sandstorm threatened, Mama would call them in: "Hoo! *Hoo!* Girls!" Everyone hurried to untie the canvas flaps above the screens. Emily and Helen could reach the knots if they stood on chairs. A wooden slat at the bottom of each flap dropped heavily—snapping the canvas tight, keeping out the blowing sand.

Jane worried a lot. "What if we get sick out here? What if a rattlesnake bites us?"

"There's a syringe in the medical kit Dr. Grishaw gave me," Mama reassured her. "I can give you a shot to keep the poison from hurting you." After that, Emily was extra careful about snakes. Papa had explained that rattlesnake bites usually didn't kill you, just made you sick. Emily wasn't really afraid of snakes. Mama with that needle, though—that was another matter.

That fall Papa managed to buy a stripped-down Ford to drive to work, so Mama could take the girls to school in the Dodge. "Not many families have two cars," Emily told Jane. "It's like being rich."

"Hardly," said Jane. Jane never invited her friends to the ranch. She didn't say why. Emily thought it might be because of the outhouse.

Well, Emily's friend Sarah didn't mind the outhouse. She even came to spend the night. Emily showed her how to prime the pump with a half bucket of water. Everybody clapped when Sarah finally brought a stream of water coughing and sputtering from the pump. Mama brewed tea from it with lots of hot milk and plenty of sugar, and she poured it from the Van Kleeck silver teapot.

After supper Papa let Emily and Sarah have target practice with him, shooting
a real rifle. As the sun set, they walked between the rows of milo maize Mr. Prest
had helped to plant. Emily told Sarah about how the whole desert was going to
blossom as the rose.

A few days before Christmas Papa bought an old mantel from the lumberyard and nailed it to one wall, so they'd have a place to hang their stockings. Mama helped them make wreaths from greasewood.

They put one over the mantel and one on the door, and carried the other two over to Mr. and Mrs. Prest, for presents. The Prests came over to their house on Christmas eve, and everyone squeezed in around the piano to sing carols. Mama had baked mince pies, so the house smelled like Christmas.

Later, they walked the Prests halfway home. "The stars over Bethlehem must have blazed this brightly," said Papa, looking up into the desert sky.

On the way back Jane whispered fiercely to Emily, "This is the first year I can remember that we didn't have a Christmas tree." She sighed, and after a moment added, "I know there wasn't room. But two more years of this!"

It seemed like a good Christmas to Emily, but she knew better than to say that to Jane. She just held her sister's hand the rest of the way.

Spring was starting when Emily heard Mama singing, a song she used to sing in the old house. "Won't you come home, Bill Bailey, won't you come home," she sang. At supper that evening she told Papa a letter had come from Cousin Fletcher, back east. He wanted to lend them money so that they could buy the land outright, instead of having to homestead it. "I'm sure that Mr. Prest would tend the crops for us," said Mama. "If you feel you'd like to move back to town, the house is only leased out until June. We could."

Emily knew Jane was hoping Papa would say yes. Carol probably wouldn't notice where she lived as long as there were plenty of books around; Helen was too little to care. Emily wasn't sure what she hoped, herself. She missed their old house too. But she wanted to be there when the desert blossomed as a rose.

By the next morning, though, Papa had decided that maybe he did need more time in town. He was busy trying to get the state to set aside money for education. "This isn't wild frontier anymore," he would tell people. "It's time we were building some colleges."

Emily never knew just when Papa finally sold the land to Mr. Prest.

When Emily and Jane were grandmothers, they made a trip together back to their hometown. About two miles west of the college they found the spot where their ranch had been. At the top of the mesa they got out of the car, and stood looking down on orchards and fields watered green by the waters of the rivers. "If only Papa could have seen this!" said Jane at last.

Emily had to smile.

"This is what he always saw," she told her sister.

Oddly enough, my mother never told me of how in 1919 her father tried to homestead a tract of land some seven miles east of Yuma, Arizona. Only in recent years, and from the unpublished memories of my aunt Tahe—the family nickname for Frances Doan Turner—did I learn of that chapter of our family history. Tahe's account made me ponder the character of a grandfather who died before I could know him, and wonder how that year might have seemed to others in his family. While my own text draws from details of those experiences described by my aunt, its characters have of course wandered from their models in family history, and become mixed with imagination.

Today the valley my grandfather viewed from his ranch is as verdant as Papa's dreams. Arizona Western College stands on the broad mesa a few miles from where the little Doan girls once chased tennis balls across the sand.

Too many of us never try seriously to realize our dreams. I have a certain weakness for those who dream big dreams and are willing to risk failure in their pursuit. I hope my grandfather was not too different from the Papa of this story.